GARFIELD

at the Gym

Lazy Fat Cat

Created by Jim Davis
Story by Jim Kraft

Illustrated by Mike Fentz

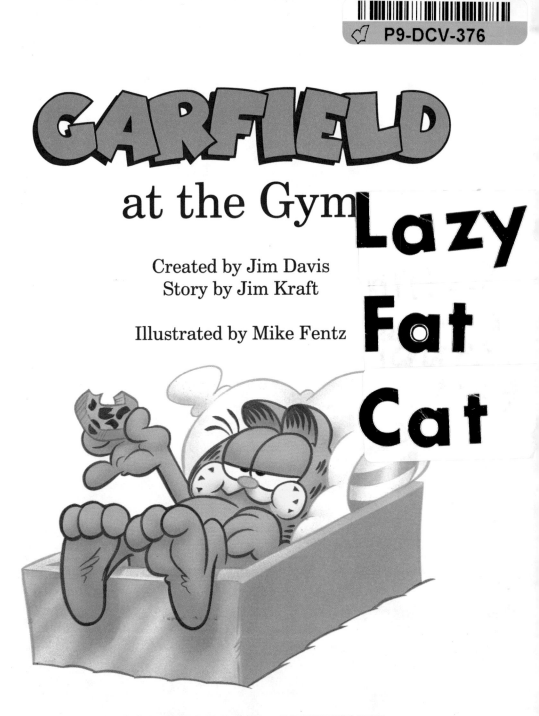

A GOLDEN BOOK • NEW YORK

Western Publishing Company, Inc., Racine, Wisconsin 53404

**and
Garfield**

One day Jon said,
"We are too soft, Garfield.
We eat too much.
We sit too much."
"And *you* talk too much,"
said Garfield.

3

"Let's work out at the gym,"
said Jon.
"We will feel better.
We will sleep better."
"I will see you later,"
said Garfield.

Garfield tried to run away.
"You are very slow,"
said Jon.
"I am very tired,"
said Garfield.

Jon took Garfield
to the gym.
"This place is great,"
said Jon.
"This will be fun."

9

First Jon rode the bike.
"Ride, Jon! Ride!"
cried Garfield.

12

Then Jon tried the rower.
"Row, Jon! Row!"
cried Garfield.

14

Jon tried to lift something.
It was very heavy—
thanks to Garfield!
"Lift, Jon! Lift!"
said Garfield.

16

Then Jon jumped into the pool.
"Swim, Jon! Swim!"
said Garfield.
"And watch out for sharks!"

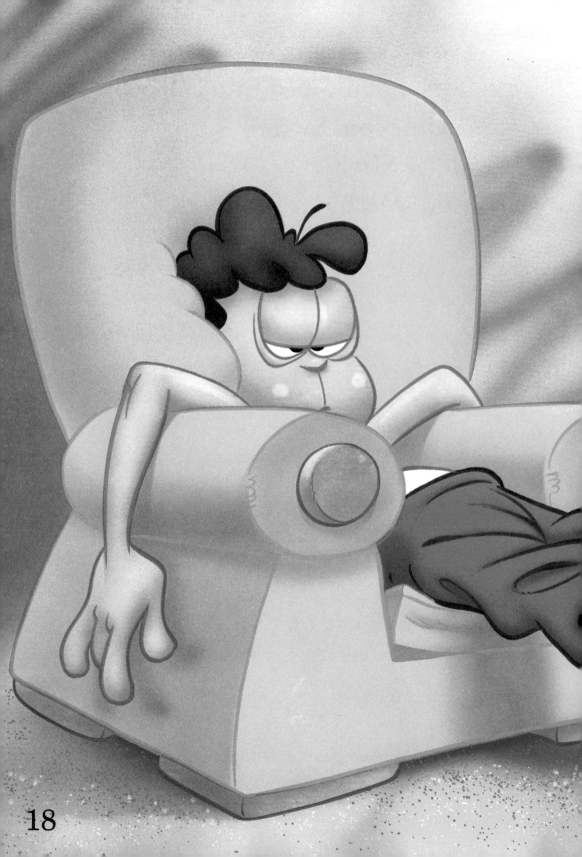

At last they went home.
"I am tired," said Jon.
"Working out is hard work.
But not for *you*, Garfield.
You did not work out."

"I will work out *my* way,"
said Garfield.
"I will show you.

"First, I warm up
my fingers and toes.
Like this," said Garfield.

"Then I play catch.

"I go for a swim.

"Then I do sit-ups,"
said Garfield.
"I sit up and watch TV.

"Next I jog—to the kitchen.

"Then I lift something heavy.

"I top it off with
a long jump.
Now *that* is what
I call working out,"
said Garfield.

30

"That is not working out,"
said Jon.
"That is not good for you.
You are still soft."

"You are right, Jon,"
said Garfield,
eating a cookie.
"I am still soft.
And I will work hard
to stay that way!"